HENRY

JAMES

PERCY

MEET ALL THESE FRIENDS IN BUZZ BOOKS:

Thomas the Tank Engine
The Animals of Farthing Wood
Biker Mice from Mars
Winnie-the-Pooh
Fireman Sam
Rupert
Babar

First published in Great Britain 1990 by Buzz Books
an imprint of Reed Children's Books
Michelin House, 81 Fulham Road, London SW3 6RB
and Auckland, Melbourne, Singapore and Toronto
Reprinted 1992, 1994, 1995

Copyright © William Heinemann Limited 1990
All publishing rights: William Heinemann Ltd
All television and merchandising rights
licensed by William Heinemann Limited to
Britt Allcroft (Thomas) Limited, exclusively, worldwide

Photographs © Britt Allcroft (Thomas) Ltd 1985, 1986
Photographs by David Mitton, Kenny McArthur and
Terry Permane for Britt Allcroft's production of
Thomas the Tank Engine and Friends

ISBN 1 85591 024 1

Printed and bound in Italy by Olivotto

GORDON OFF THE RAILS

buzz books

Gordon was resting in a siding. Sometimes, when he was resting, he would say to himself, "It's really *very* tiring to be such a large and splendid engine. One does have to keep up appearances so."

At that moment Henry came by. "Peep, peep! Peep, peep! Hello, Fatface!" whistled

6

Henry. Gordon had not seen Henry for some time.

"What a cheek!" he spluttered. "That Henry is getting too big for his wheels. Fancy speaking to me like that! *Meeee*!" he went on, letting off steam. "*Meee* who has never had an accident!"

Percy heard Gordon's last remark and he knew that it wasn't true.

"Aren't burst safety valves accidents?" Percy asked, innocently.

Gordon was very cross. He didn't like being teased and he knew that Percy was talking about the time when he, Gordon, had pulled the express too fast and had burst a safety valve.

"No indeed! High spirits! Might happen to any engine!" replied Gordon, huffily. "But, to come off the rails like Henry did when he was pulling *The Flying Kipper* . . . well, I ask you!" he went on. "Is it right? Is it decent?"

A few days later it was Henry's turn to take the express. Gordon watched him getting ready.

"Be careful, Henry," he said. "You're not pulling *The Flying Kipper* now! Mind you keep on the rails today!"

Henry snorted away. Gordon yawned and went to sleep.

But he didn't sleep for very long.

"Wake up, Gordon!" said his driver.
"A special train is coming in and we're to
pull it."

"Is it coaches or trucks?" asked Gordon,
sleepily.

"Trucks," said his driver.

"Trucks!" said Gordon, crossly. "Pah!"

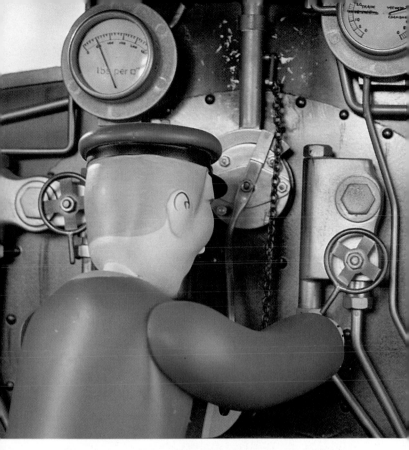

The men lit Gordon's fire and oiled him
ready for the run.

He needed to go on the turntable first so
that he would be facing the right way.

His fire was slow to start and wouldn't
burn.

They couldn't wait so Edward was called to help Gordon to the turntable.

"I won't go. I won't go," grumbled Gordon.

"Don't be silly. Don't be silly," puffed Edward.

At last Gordon was on the turntable. Edward was uncoupled and he backed away.

Gordon's driver and fireman jumped down to turn him round.

The movement had shaken Gordon's fire so that it was soon burning nicely.

Gordon was cross and he didn't care what he did. He waited until the table was halfway round and then his chance came. "I'll show them! I'll show them!" he hissed.

He moved slowly forward. He only meant to go a little way – just far enough to 'jam' the turntable and stop it turning.

But his plan was going wrong – he couldn't stop himself . . .

He slithered and slipped off the rails, down the embankment and settled in a ditch.

"OOOOOsh!" he hissed. "Get me out! Get me out!" he called.

His driver and fireman came to see him.

"Not a hope," said his driver.
"You're stuck, you silly great engine, don't you understand that?"

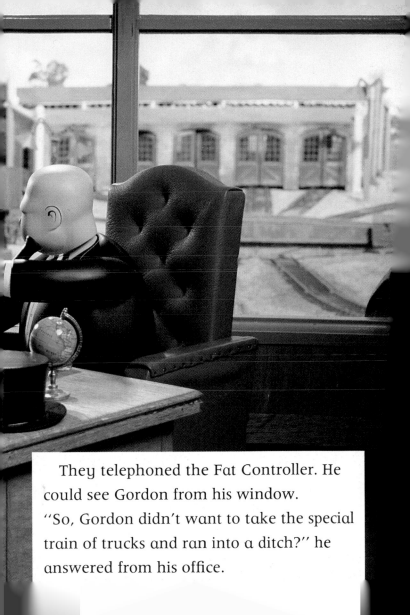

They telephoned the Fat Controller. He could see Gordon from his window.

"So, Gordon didn't want to take the special train of trucks and ran into a ditch?" he answered from his office.

"What's that you say?" he went on.
"The special's waiting – well, tell Edward to take it, please. And Gordon? Oh, leave him where he is. We haven't time to bother with him now!"

So there was Gordon, stuck in the ditch. Over on the other side, some little boys were chattering. "Coo!" they called. "Doesn't he look silly! They'll never get him out."

Then the boys began to sing:
Silly old Gordon fell in a ditch,
fell in a ditch,
fell in a ditch.
Silly old Gordon fell in a ditch,
all on a Monday morning!

Gordon lay in the ditch all day.
"Oh dear!" he thought. "I shall never get
out."

But that evening the men brought floodlights. They used powerful jacks to lift Gordon and made a road of sleepers under his wheels to keep him out of the mud.

Strong wire ropes were fastened to his back end and James and Henry, pulling hard, at last managed to bring Gordon back to the rails.

Late that night Gordon crawled home, a sadder and wiser engine.

THOMAS

EDWARD

GORDON